Once upon a time there lived a shoemaker with his wife in a large town. He was honest and hardworking. But no one bought the shoes he made. The shoemaker worked harder yet it became difficult for him to even earn a square meal for his family!

Finally, the shoemaker was left with just enough leather to make only one pair of shoes. "I can cut only one pair of shoes out of this leather," he told his wife, sadly. "Don't worry, something good will surely happen," replied his wife.

The shoemaker cut out the last pair of shoes and went home. The next morning, when the shoemaker walked into his shop, he was surprised.

On the table, were kept a pair of beautiful shoes. "What a beautiful pair of shoes!" exclaimed the shoemaker and rushed towards the table. He picked up the beautiful pair of shoes and wondered, "Who could have made these shoes?"

Few minutes later his wife came to the shop. "Look, someone has made such beautiful shoes out of the leather which I had cut last night," the shoemaker said to his wife. "I can't believe my eyes!" cried his wife who was equally surprised and happy to see the beautiful pair of shoes.

As the shoemaker and his wife stood admiring the pair of shoes, a merchant was passing by. He saw the beautiful shoes and thought, 'Those shoes are beautiful indeed. I must buy them for my wife.'

He stood at the entrance of the shoemaker's shop and said, "Sir, I would like to buy this pair of beautiful shoes." He offered two gold coins to the shoemaker. The shoemaker happily agreed. The merchant took the shoes, thanked the shoemaker and went away. "This money is enough to buy leather for two pairs of shoes," said the shoemaker, happily.

That day, the shoemaker bought leather enough to make two pairs of shoes. "Who do you think has helped us?" asked the shoemaker's wife as the shoemaker was cutting out the leather to make the next two pairs of shoes. "I don't know, but I am grateful for his help," replied the shoemaker.

As was the practice also, the shoemaker left the cut leather pieces for two pairs of shoes on the table. "I will make the shoes tomorrow," said the shoemaker and went home.

Next morning, to their surprise, two pairs of beautiful shoes lay on the table like the previous day. "Someone has again made the shoes," said the shoemaker. Soon, those two pairs of shoes were also sold. In this manner, everyday when the shoemaker left the leather cut out for the shoes in his shop, the next morning he found that the shoes were ready!

Soon, the shoemaker became rich. One day, his wife said, "I think we should find out the person who has been helping us all this while." "You are right! Let's hide in the shop tonight and find out," replied the shoemaker.

The shoemaker and his wife hid themselves behind the curtains that night. Suddenly, at the stroke of midnight, two elves hopped in through the window. They were tiny creatures in torn clothes. Quickly, they picked up the leather pieces and began to work.

Once, the shoes were ready, the elves hopped out from the window. "We must thank these little elves who have helped us in our difficult times," said the shoemaker's wife. "What should we do to show our gratitude to these little elves?" asked the shoemaker.

The shoemaker's wife suggested that they should make tiny shoes and clothes for the little elves. "Let us begin our work right away," said the shoemaker.
Soon, the shoemaker's wife was busy stitching clothes for the elves, while the shoemaker made tiny shoes for them.

Once they were done, the shoemaker kept the shoes and clothes on the table. That night, the shoemaker did not leave any piece of leather on the table. The couple hid and waited for the elves to arrive. "I hope they like them," he said.

At midnight, the elves arrived. They were delighted to find the lovely clothes and the shoes. They put on the clothes and shoes and danced around the room. Then they hopped out of the window and disappeared.

They continued making beautiful shoes and the shoemaker became more rich and happy. The shoemaker kept his friends happy with more clothes and shoes. All lived happily ever after.